Books should be returned on or before the
last date stamped below

D0185526

First published in 1998 by Franklin Watts
96 Leonard Street, London EC2A 4XD

Franklin Watts Australia
56 O'Riordan Street, Alexandria, Sydney, NSW 2015

This edition published 2002
Text © Michael Lawrence 1998

The right of Michael Lawrence to be identified as the
Author of this Work has been asserted by him in
accordance with the Copyright, Designs and Patents Act,
1988

Editor: Matthew Parselle
Series Editor: Paula Borton
Designer: Kirstie Billingham
Consultant: Dr Anne Millard, BA Hons, Dip Ed, PhD

A CIP catalogue record for this book
is available from the British Library.

ISBN 0 7496 4594 6 (pbk)

Dewey Classification 822.3

Printed in Great Britain

Mystery at the Globe

by
Michael Lawrence

Illustrations by Julie Anderson

W

FRANKLIN WATTS
NEW YORK • LONDON • SYDNEY

For Martin Gee

1

Down With the Theatre!

Judith Shakespeare stared in horror at the bare timbers, spindly and stark against the cold December sky; the dozens of men scrambling like ants over what little was left of the once impressive building.

"Father! What's going on?"

Will Shakespeare eyed her with amusement. "I should have mentioned it in my last letter, but the decision was made almost before we knew it ourselves. We're pulling it down, Judith. Taking the old theatre apart piece by piece and rebuilding it elsewhere."

He saw the disappointment on his daughter's face. Newly arrived from Stratford to spend Christmas with him in

London, she'd been looking forward
to being entertained here over the
festive season.

"We had no choice, my love. The
landlord flatly refuses to renew the lease
on the land, yet the building belongs to
the company. So we're moving on, and
taking it with us."

"And what does the landlord have to
say about that?"

Her father winked at her.
"He doesn't know.
He's away up north,
won't be back till
after Christmas –
which is why
we're in such a
hurry here." He
stepped up on to
his ladder,

chuckling. "Miserable old devil's in for quite a shock."

"He certainly is," Judith murmured.

"Well, I must get on. We'll have a good old chinwag later, I promise, but for now... Look, there's young Nathan. Why don't you go and have a chat with him?"

Still a little dazed, Judith drifted over to the cart that Nathan Field was loading timbers onto.

Nathan's face lit up when she asked him what he thought of this mad scheme.

"I think it's brilliant. And your father says I can start playing bigger parts once the new place is up. Mostly female roles still, but it's a step forward."

"You don't know how lucky you are," Judith said wistfully. "I'd love to go on the stage."

Nathan smirked. "Girls can't act! They wouldn't know where to start."

She glared at him. "They're never given the chance. It's so stupid, boys playing female parts when they'd be played so much better by –"

She was cut short by a loud shout.

A small group of men were marching towards the remains of the theatre, led by a fat red-faced man waving a sheet of paper over his head.

"I have here an order from the owner commanding you to cease this wholesale destruction of his property."

"Someone must have sent word," Nathan muttered grimly. "Now we're for it."

The men on the ladders and scaffolding looked at one another, not sure what to do. Several dropped to the ground, Will Shakespeare among them, and the Burbage brothers, Cuthbert and Richard. Cuthbert examined the landlord's order, but Richard had  no intention of reading it.

"My father built this place from his own purse 25 years ago, and with the landowner's agreement," he said. "It was my father's property, and now that he's dead it belongs to my brother and me. And we, sir, are determined to have it for our own use, so why don't you run along and tell your master that?"

The landlord's agent scowled. "Very well, if that's your attitude you leave me no choice." He turned to his men. "You know what to do."

The agent's men drew their swords and moved towards the building. They didn't get far. As if a whispered message had flown from ear to ear around the site, several dozen workers stepped out to meet them, and in a trice the agent's men stood within a semi-circle of axes and hammers and hefty lengths of wood that would do their skulls no good at all.

"I wouldn't if I were you," one of the workers warned. He was a tall thin fellow with a wispy beard and a wide mouth that was quick to smile, even when making a threat.

"Who's that?" Judith whispered to Nathan.

"Edmund Nashe," he hissed back. "One of the clowns. He acts a bit too."

"A clown! I've never seen such a cruel face."

"Listen, we don't want any trouble," one of the landlord's men was saying.

"We're just doing our job."

"Yes, well it will be a happier day for you," Edmund Nashe replied, "if you do it somewhere else. Unless, that is, you fancy going home bruised and battered from head to foot."

The agent fumed, but saw that he stood no chance against these people. "You haven't heard the last of this," he huffed, and stalked away. His men followed him, bashfully sheathing their swords.

The company of actors and their hirelings cheered, but Will Shakespeare and the Burbage brothers exchanged nervous glances. Could they really have got away with it so easily? They resolved to keep their wits about them, just in case.

2

Across the Thames

Needing to occupy herself, Judith set to
work with the others, numbering the
timbers that were handed down and
helping to carry them to the waiting carts.
When a cart was full it was driven
southward, through the city gates,

across London. Judith went with one of the last carts of the day, sitting on the piled wood picking splinters out of her palms and thinking that whatever her expectations of this Christmas, delights like this had not been among them.

The site chosen for the new theatre was at Southwark, on the other side of the river. The plan had been to cart the timbers across London Bridge, but so cold had it been of late that the Thames had frozen over, so they pushed them across the ice instead.

This wasn't easy until you found your ice-feet, as Judith soon learnt to her cost. She was pushing her first timber away

from the bank
when her feet
suddenly whipped
away from her as
if tugged by an
invisible hand. Down she
went, flat on her back, all the breath
knocked out of her.

"Allow me, madam!"

And just as suddenly she was being
helped up – by Edmund Nashe, the actor-
clown, who'd driven up in the next cart

just as she was stepping onto the ice.
How he'd reached her so quickly was
beyond her.

"I... thank you," she said, flustered.

A smile twitched across Nashe's
expressive lips. A very broad smile.
He bowed low before her.

"My pleasure,
lady!"

His voice was
as icy as the Thames, his words
mildly mocking, and when he straightened
up he gazed at her with the blackest eyes
she'd ever seen. But then, with as little
warning as he'd given of his arrival, this

alarming man
somersaulted
backwards and
walked away
on his hands,
giving a tiny
comic yelp
with each
step to show
how cold the
ice was.
Judith was
more than a
little relieved
to see him go.

On the south bank of the river, the
building of the theatre was already well
underway, with the newly-arrived timbers
stacked all around the site. Local
householders and shopkeepers stood

watching the work in progress, muttering among themselves.

"Haven't we got enough of these theatres? There's already the Swan and the Rose this side of the river, what do we want another one for?"

"Actors! Idle good-for-nothings, wastrels. I'd horsewhip 'em, that's what I'd do. Send 'em packing with a flea in their ear."

When her father joined her at Southwark in the dark early evening,

Judith asked him how long he thought it would take to build the new theatre.

"Well, if the weather's kind to us," – he glanced at the bleak winter sky – "I reckon we could be open by mid-April. Always supposing our friend doesn't stick a few extra spokes in our wheels, that is."

He meant their old landlord, of course. "But what can he do once all the timbers have been removed from his land?" Judith asked.

Will's face was grubby, his hair wild, his clothes torn here and there, and he was enjoying himself enormously. He gave her an impish grin.

"If I knew that I wouldn't be an actor and scribbler of plays, I'd be a fortune-teller – and no doubt make my fortune into the bargain. But if I know nothing else, I know that that man is capable of anything. Absolutely anything. I wouldn't trust him an inch."

3

The Maggot

Judith was back home in Stratford two days
after Christmas. Home was a pretty house
of brick and timber called New Place, which
she shared with her mother and her older
sister Susanna – and her father whenever
he could tear himself away from London.

Will did not come near Stratford for
the whole of the winter, but then, one day
early in May, a letter arrived inviting them

to the opening of
the new theatre –
the Globe, as it
was to be called.
Judith was
thrilled, but
Susanna,
who had no
interest in
her father's
work, sniffed
and said, "I have more important things
to think about than plays and theatres,"
while their mother began fretting about
being away from home and in any case
being "no great one for cities". So once
again Judith went without them.

Her excitement grew as she approached
Southwark, and she clapped her hands with
delight when she had her first sight of the
new theatre. Towering above the
neighbouring houses, shops, inns and places
of business, its white walls glowing in the
soft May light, the Globe
looked magnificent.

A juggler was strutting about in the cobbled forecourt, tossing apples and daggers hand to hand before a gathering crowd. Judith recognised him at once. It was the clown, the acrobatic actor who

had helped her up from the ice on her last visit – Edmund Nashe.

When Nashe tossed one of the apples high into the air all eyes followed it; followed too the dagger that he sent in pursuit. When the apple reached its highest point the dagger caught up with it and skewered it clean through. The apple spun awkwardly, the point of the blade embedded in it, and tumbled earthward, until the knife's handle landed with a soft slap in the juggler's open palm.

The spectators applauded and whistled and Nashe bowed extravagantly. Then – suddenly – he spun smartly on his heel and faced Judith. Judith gasped in shock, which seemed to amuse Nashe. He smiled that long cruel smile of his and offered her the apple on the tip of his dagger.

"Your servant, mistress! Eat! Be merry!"

Judith flushed as all heads turned her way, but accepted the apple out of courtesy. Nashe swept the cobbles with his sleeve, took several backward steps, still bowing low, and vanished into the crowd.

Judith turned the apple over nervously as if expecting it to burst into flames or become something other than what it appeared to be. It was hard and green and smooth, flawless but for the knife's cut. An ordinary apple, nothing more. But as she gazed at it, something moved

in the cut. She peered closer. A maggot poked its head out.

"Eeeergg!"

She threw the apple from her in disgust.

"Judith – there you are!"

Her father had just stepped out of a small side door and was coming towards her, beaming. She rushed to him. They embraced, exchanged greetings; then Will turned her to face the new building.

"Well, what do you think? Come on now, your honest opinion."

"I think," Judith said softly, "that you've built the finest theatre in London. Probably the world."

"That's what I think too," he said, and squeezed her delightedly.

"We would have opened sooner, but there have been a few... mishaps."

"Mishaps? What sort of mishaps? You didn't mention anything in your letters."

"I didn't want your mother worrying.

You know what she's like, fuss, fuss, fuss at the drop of a hat."

"Tell me now then," Judith said.

"Well, they started back in February. A mysteriously falling beam that broke a man's arm, solid floors that suddenly gave way, a bout of stomach cramps that laid half the company low for the better part of a week. That sort of thing."

"Quite a lot of bad luck," Judith said.

"Luck? Oh, I doubt that luck, good or

bad, had much to do with it. Especially as a week before the problems started our old landlord stumped up demanding a share of the profits. We'd stolen his theatre, he said, and deprived him of a part of his income. The only profit he got from us was a barrage of boots up the bottom."

"So you think it was all his doing?"

"Of course!" Will replied cheerfully. "Too many coincidences otherwise."

"I suppose so," Judith said. "But tell me, have you written a new play for the opening?"

"I would have, but I don't seem to have had the time somehow. So we're opening with A Midsummer Night's Dream. Always goes down well, that one."

He noticed Nathan Field loitering nearby and called him over. "I've given young Nathan a good part in our first production, haven't I lad?"

Nathan muttered something that Judith didn't quite catch. She asked him to repeat it, but Will answered for him – rather more loudly than was necessary.

"He's playing Titania, Queen of the Fairies!"

A man passing by hooted with laughter and Nathan went bright red and wriggled with embarrassment.

"I hope he's not going to disappoint me," Will added, and leaned towards Nathan. "I want no mistakes. Not a word or pause or flutter of fairy wings out of place – understand?"

Nathan again mumbled something.

"If you have trouble learning your lines," Will went on, "you might ask Judith – she knows my stuff almost by heart."

"So I do," Judith said. "I could play Titania standing on my head."

Will raised an eyebrow at her. "Yes, and very amusing it would be, but it's Nathan who's playing her, and he's

playing her on his feet." He turned back to Nathan. "Off with you, lad, while I give this young lady a guided tour of our little playhouse."

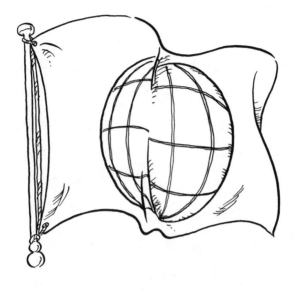

4

Fire!

Come the big day everyone was on edge,
especially Nathan, by then a bag of nerves
at the thought of playing the Queen of
the Fairies to an audience of two thousand
or more.

"I'd give anything for a male part," he

confided to Judith, "even a small one like Edmund's. I know his lines better than my own."

Judith watched Edmund Nashe practising somersaults and handstands. His part in the play was small because he had the job of

keeping the audience amused between acts. Audiences got very restless if nothing happened for more than a minute at a time.

Long before the performance started, the theatre was packed from floor to ceiling. Even the "pit", the area before the stage, was full of standing spectators. When the first act came to an end, all colour drained from Nathan's face. He was to make his first appearance in the second act.

"All set, Nathan?" Will said, clapping him on the shoulder.

"No," Nathan answered miserably.

"Good lad. Oh, Judith, would you run up to the roof for me? I think I left Titania's wand in the turret when I was up there earlier. Nathan's going to need it."

"What on earth were you doing up there with Titania's wand?" Judith asked.

"Casting a spell that all would be well today. It seems to have worked!" He walked off chuckling.

Judith climbed the three flights of stairs. The turret was where the flag was run up, the enormous flag with the Globe's emblem that would inform London that a play was about to start. To her surprise, she found that on this of all days no one had remembered to raise the flag. It lay neatly folded on the floor near Titania's wand, which had rolled between the floorboards.

She was about to go back down with the wand when she heard a roar from the crowd below.

The spectators in the pit had pushed back to make room for Edmund Nashe, who had somersaulted into their midst and was now strutting about on his hands waggling his toes in the air. From her high vantage point, Judith watched as Nashe flipped himself upright and lit several torches from a flame provided by an assistant. When he began to juggle with the flaming torches the audience was clearly impressed. One slip and he might burn himself badly.

When one of the torches

suddenly left Nashe's hand and flew up towards the roof, Judith was reminded of the apple that he'd thrown shortly after her arrival – and the maggot within it. Up flew the torch, up and up and up, until it passed so close to her that she felt its warmth.

Reaching its furthest limit some way above her head, the torch turned over to begin its descent – but then something terrible happened.

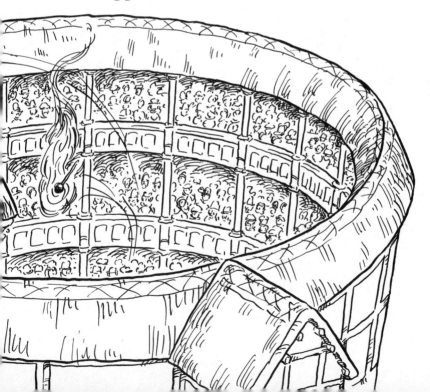

The weight of the handle threw the torch off balance and instead of plummeting earthward to land four square in the juggler's palm, it skewed sideways and tumbled onto the dry reeds of the thatched roof.

Judith gulped. The roof formed a complete circle round the top of the building. If the flames spread they would swiftly follow the circle in both directions until the roof was ablaze at every point. Then the timbers below would catch, and in minutes the entire theatre would be engulfed in flames, and hundreds of people, struggling to escape via the two exit points, might be trapped

in the burning building – doomed to a
horrible death.

She stared down past the sputtering
roof. Everyone was looking up, wondering
what had happened to the torch; everyone
except Edmund
Nashe, who had
mysteriously
disappeared.

Then someone spotted the amber flame
nibbling at the lower edge of the thatch.

"Look! Fire!"

A cry at once echoed in all parts of
the building.

"Fire! Fire!"

Panic gripped the audience. The Globe resounded with shouts, yells, shrieks, as people flung themselves down the stairs, fighting to get out. Only one tried to get up instead of down – Will Shakespeare, bellowing "Judith! Judith!" – but he was unable to get through, and the downward push carried him helplessly before it, shouting his daughter's name over and over again.

And above all this, in the most dangerous spot of all, Judith realized with a sharp pang of terror that she alone was in a position to save the new theatre. The right position, but could she do it? There was no time to think. She must act, before fear had time to set in.

She pounced on the forgotten flag, unfurled it, cast it upon the flames just below her. Then she hauled herself up on

the ledge and jumped. She landed full
length on the flag, and set about beating it
with her open hands.

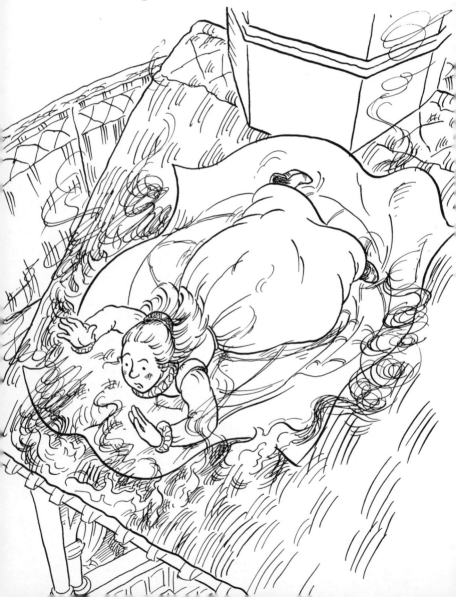

5

"That Lad Will Go Far..."

Nathan had slipped outside to try and calm himself before the second act. When Edmund Nashe shot through the door he went flying over the Fairy Queen's outstretched legs, cracked his head on the corner of a bench, and was knocked cold.

The horrified Nathan was bent over
Nashe, trying to revive him, when the
audience began rushing out, along with
a furious Richard Burbage looking for
"that lunatic with the torches". So dizzy
was Nashe when he opened his eyes that

he addressed Burbage by the old landowner's name, adding – "I've done your bidding, sir, I've destroyed the Globe. Now pay me the agreed sum, or..."

Too late he realized who was standing over him, and that the game was up.

"So," Burbage growled. "It was you!"

There had been a traitor in their midst all this time, paid by their old landlord to first make life difficult for the company, then burn the theatre to the ground.

It escaped no one that Judith had single-handedly saved the Globe – and a great many lives – though there was the odd grumble about her having ruined the company's nice new flag.

When some sort of reward was proposed, Judith's eyes sparkled.

"There's only one reward I want," she said.

Everyone was shocked when she told them what it was, but agreed to it on the understanding that it was kept a secret from the outside world.

"And just the once, mind," her father said to her. "Once and once only, Judith. There'll be no making a habit of it."

So shaken were the players by the near disaster that the opening performance was cancelled, but when A Midsummer Night's Dream was staged the following day the small role that was to have been played by the treacherous

Edmund Nashe was played instead by Nathan Field. Nathan was delighted. His first adult male part! But the star of the production was Titania, Queen of the Fairies. "That lad can act!" the audience was heard to murmur. "He'll go far." The "lad" did not go far, but it was with great pride that Judith took a graceful bow at the end of her one and only stage performance.

And she never told anyone, not even
her mother and sister when she returned to
Stratford a week later, that she had
been the first ever actress in a
Shakespeare play.

Notes

The first real theatre

Before the first theatres were built in 16th century England, companies of actors performed in the yards of inns, and the streets, passing the hat round for pennies. One such company was managed by a carpenter turned actor called James Burbage. In the mid-1570s Burbage leased some land at Shoreditch, just north of London, and built the first proper theatre, which he called

The Theatre. This was the building that Burbage's sons Richard and Cuthbert, with Will Shakespeare and other friends, pulled down and carried to Southwark over Christmas 1598.

Spending a penny (or three)

People paid a penny to get into the Globe, another penny if they wanted to sit down, and a third for one of the best seats, with cushions.

The burning of the Globe

The Globe really did burn down some years after this story takes place, during a performance of Shakespeare's Henry VIII, in which Richard Burbage played the king. A spark from a cannon set off during

the play set fire to the thatched roof and the building burned to the ground in less than an hour. Everyone managed to escape, though one man's trousers caught fire (he put it out with a bottle of ale, apparently). The Globe was rebuilt the following year – this time with a tiled roof!

Queen Elizabeth I

Queen Elizabeth was a great fan of Shakespeare's plays, but she didn't go to the theatre to see them

like ordinary people. The actors performed for
her at one or another of her palaces. When
Elizabeth died in 1603 and James I came to the
throne, the Chamberlain's Men (as the company
was called) were renamed the King's Men at
his request.

Judith

Judith Shakespeare was
born in 1585. She had a
twin brother called Hamnet,
who died in 1596, aged
eleven. Judith married in
February 1616. Her
husband, Thomas
Quiney, seems to
have had eyes for
other ladies as well as her. This may have been
why, shortly after the wedding, her father made a
new will which made sure that Judith, while not
inheriting a fortune, would at least have enough to
live on if her husband left her.

Retirement in Stratford

By the time William Shakespeare retired to New Place in or about 1610 he'd made enough money from his plays to live the life of a country gentleman. He seems to have stopped writing altogether once he retired. He died on 23rd April 1616, aged 52 – about two months after Judith's marriage.

Nathan Field – actor and playwright

There may not have been a
boy called Nathan Field in
the Chamberlain's Men
in 1598-9, but Will Shakespeare did have an old
Stratford friend named Richard Field, who moved
to London and became a successful printer. And in
1616, the very year of Will's death, a young actor
and playwright named Nathan Field joined the
King's Men...

A Globe for today

In 1997, almost four hundred years after the first
Globe was built at Southwark, a new Globe opened
very near the original site. This was the brainchild of
American actor and director Sam Wanamaker, who
made sure that the Globe of our time looks and feels
as much as possible like the Globe built by Will
Shakespeare and his friends in the reign of the first
Queen Elizabeth. It's well worth a visit.

Sparks: Historical Adventures

ANCIENT GREECE
The Great Horse of Troy – The Trojan War
0 7496 3369 7 (hbk)   0 7496 3538 X (pbk)
The Winner's Wreath – Ancient Greek Olympics
0 7496 3368 9 (hbk)   0 7496 3555 X (pbk)

INVADERS AND SETTLERS
Boudicca Strikes Back – The Romans in Britain
0 7496 3366 2 (hbk)   0 7496 3546 0 (pbk)
Viking Raiders – A Norse Attack
0 7496 3089 2 (hbk)   0 7496 3457 X (pbk)
Erik's New Home – A Viking Town
0 7496 3367 0 (hbk)   0 7496 3552 5 (pbk)
TALES OF THE ROWDY ROMANS
The Great Necklace Hunt
0 7496 2221 0 (hbk)   0 7496 2628 3 (pbk)
The Lost Legionary
0 7496 2222 9 (hbk)   0 7496 2629 1 (pbk)
The Guard Dog Geese
0 7496 2331 4 (hbk)   0 7496 2630 5 (pbk)
A Runaway Donkey
0 7496 2332 2 (hbk)   0 7496 2631 3 (pbk)

TUDORS AND STUARTS
Captain Drake's Orders – The Armada
0 7496 2556 2 (hbk)   0 7496 3121 X (pbk)
London's Burning – The Great Fire of London
0 7496 2557 0 (hbk)   0 7496 3122 8 (pbk)
Mystery at the Globe – Shakespeare's Theatre
0 7496 3096 5 (hbk)   0 7496 3449 9 (pbk)
Plague! – A Tudor Epidemic
0 7496 3365 4 (hbk)   0 7496 3556 8 (pbk)
Stranger in the Glen – Rob Roy
0 7496 2586 4 (hbk)   0 7496 3123 6 (pbk)
A Dream of Danger – The Massacre of Glencoe
0 7496 2587 2 (hbk)   0 7496 3124 4 (pbk)
A Queen's Promise – Mary Queen of Scots
0 7496 2589 9 (hbk)   0 7496 3125 2 (pbk)
Over the Sea to Skye – Bonnie Prince Charlie
0 7496 2588 0 (hbk)   0 7496 3126 0 (pbk)
TALES OF A TUDOR TEARAWAY
A Pig Called Henry
0 7496 2204 4 (hbk)   0 7496 2625 9 (pbk)
A Horse Called Deathblow
0 7496 2205 9 (hbk)   0 7496 2624 0 (pbk)
Dancing for Captain Drake
0 7496 2234 2 (hbk)   0 7496 2626 7 (pbk)
Birthdays are a Serious Business
0 7496 2235 0 (hbk)   0 7496 2627 5 (pbk)

VICTORIAN ERA
The Runaway Slave – The British Slave Trade
0 7496 3093 0 (hbk)   0 7496 3456 1 (pbk)
The Sewer Sleuth – Victorian Cholera
0 7496 2590 2 (hbk)   0 7496 3128 7 (pbk)
Convict! – Criminals Sent to Australia
0 7496 2591 0 (hbk)   0 7496 3129 5 (pbk)
An Indian Adventure – Victorian India
0 7496 3090 6 (hbk)   0 7496 3451 0 (pbk)
Farewell to Ireland – Emigration to America
0 7496 3094 9 (hbk)   0 7496 3448 0 (pbk)

The Great Hunger – Famine in Ireland
0 7496 3095 7 (hbk)   0 7496 3447 2 (pbk)
Fire Down the Pit – A Welsh Mining Disaster
0 7496 3091 4 (hbk)   0 7496 3450 2 (pbk)
Tunnel Rescue – The Great Western Railway
0 7496 3353 0 (hbk)   0 7496 3537 1 (pbk)
Kidnap on the Canal – Victorian Waterways
0 7496 3352 2 (hbk)   0 7496 3540 1 (pbk)
Dr. Barnardo's Boys – Victorian Charity
0 7496 3358 1 (hbk)   0 7496 3541 X (pbk)
The Iron Ship – Brunel's Great Britain
0 7496 3355 7 (hbk)   0 7496 3543 6 (pbk)
Bodies for Sale – Victorian Tomb-Robbers
0 7496 3364 6 (hbk)   0 7496 3539 8 (pbk)
Penny Post Boy – The Victorian Postal Service
0 7496 3362 X (hbk)   0 7496 3544 4 (pbk)
The Canal Diggers – The Manchester Ship Canal
0 7496 3356 5 (hbk)   0 7496 3545 2 (pbk)
The Tay Bridge Tragedy – A Victorian Disaster
0 7496 3354 9 (hbk)   0 7496 3547 9 (pbk)
Stop, Thief! – The Victorian Police
0 7496 3359 X (hbk)   0 7496 3548 7 (pbk)
Miss Buss and Miss Beale – Victorian Schools
0 7496 3360 3 (hbk)   0 7496 3549 5 (pbk)
Chimney Charlie – Victorian Chimney Sweeps
0 7496 3351 4 (hbk)   0 7496 3551 7 (pbk)
Down the Drain – Victorian Sewers
0 7496 3357 3 (hbk)   0 7496 3550 9 (pbk)
The Ideal Home – A Victorian New Town
0 7496 3361 1 (hbk)   0 7496 3553 3 (pbk)
Stage Struck – Victorian Music Hall
0 7496 3363 8 (hbk)   0 7496 3554 1 (pbk)
TRAVELS OF A YOUNG VICTORIAN
The Golden Key
0 7496 2360 8 (hbk)   0 7496 2632 1 (pbk)
Poppy's Big Push
0 7496 2361 6 (hbk)   0 7496 2633 X (pbk)
Poppy's Secret
0 7496 2374 8 (hbk)   0 7496 2634 8 (pbk)
The Lost Treasure
0 7496 2375 6 (hbk)   0 7496 2635 6 (pbk)

20th-CENTURY HISTORY
Fight for the Vote – The Suffragettes
0 7496 3092 2 (hbk)   0 7496 3452 9 (pbk)
The Road to London – The Jarrow March
0 7496 2609 7 (hbk)   0 7496 3132 5 (pbk)
The Sandbag Secret – The Blitz
0 7496 2608 9 (hbk)   0 7496 3133 3 (pbk)
Sid's War – Evacuation
0 7496 3209 7 (hbk)   0 7496 3445 6 (pbk)
D-Day! – Wartime Adventure
0 7496 3208 9 (hbk)   0 7496 3446 4 (pbk)
The Prisoner – A Prisoner of War
0 7496 3212 7 (hbk)   0 7496 3455 3 (pbk)
Escape from Germany – Wartime Refugees
0 7496 3211 9 (hbk)   0 7496 3454 5 (pbk)
Flying Bombs – Wartime Bomb Disposal
0 7496 3210 0 (hbk)   0 7496 3453 7 (pbk)
12,000 Miles From Home – Sent to Australia
0 7496 3370 0 (hbk)   0 7496 3542 8 (pbk)